Ghost Queen

MAHTAB NARSIMHAN

ORCA ANCHOR

ORCA BOOK PUBLISHERS

Published in Canada and the United States
in 2025 by Orca Book Publishers.
orcabook.com

Library and Archives Canada Cataloguing in Publication
Title: Ghost queen / Mahtab Narsimhan.
Names: Narsimhan, Mahtab, author.
Series: Orca anchor.
Description: Series statement: Orca anchor
Identifiers: Canadiana (print) 20240320697 | Canadiana (ebook) 20240320700 |
ISBN 9781459841659 (softcover) | ISBN 9781459841666 (PDF) | ISBN 9781459841673 (EPUB)
Subjects: LCGFT: Novels.
Classification: LCC PS8627.A77 G56 2025 | DDC jC813/.6—dc23

Library of Congress Control Number: 2024933247

Summary: In this high-interest accessible novel for teen readers, teen vlogger Malika and her boyfriend risk spending the night in a haunted fort in the hopes of meeting the famous ghost of a cursed Indian princess.

Orca Book Publishers is committed to reducing the consumption of nonrenewable resources in the production of our books. We make every effort to use materials that support a sustainable future.

Orca Book Publishers gratefully acknowledges the support for its publishing programs provided by the following agencies: the Government of Canada, the Canada Council for the Arts and the Province of British Columbia through the BC Arts Council and the Book Publishing Tax Credit.

Design by Ella Collier.
Edited by Gabrielle Prendergast.
Cover photography by Getty Images / David Wall.
Author photo by Shimon Karmel.

Printed and bound in Canada.

28 27 26 25 • 1 2 3 4

To Naomi

For all your support and encouragement

Chapter One

Today she would convince him. Or die trying! The monsoon season had started. Delhi was dripping. Their local dhaba was busy today. Malika sipped masala chai from a clay cup. She would have liked to be in a fancy coffee shop. She couldn't afford it. Yet.

Malika's boyfriend, Veer, scrolled through news on his phone. He helped her create content for their channel, *Ghost Queen*, on VidVibe. It was a popular platform for videos.

Veer was a knockout. All the girls in the dhaba were looking at him. And he was *her* boyfriend.

"*Ghost Queen* has 48,000 fans!" Malika said. "If we hit 50,000, we make good money. Ideas?"

Veer flashed her a warm smile. "You've already thought of an idea. Spill."

Malika blew him a kiss. He knew her well.

Ghost Queen had started the previous year. It was *her* idea. She found ghost stories to investigate. The two of them would visit the site. They'd make content for their fans.

Often the "ghost" turned out to be a trick. Wind through the trees sounding like ghostly whispers. Or an animal scream that sounded human. They hadn't found a ghost they didn't like—*yet*. But the content was fun to shoot. Their fans loved them!

"Bhangarh Fort!" Malika said.

"NO!" Veer said. "It's the most haunted place in India. And it's in Rajasthan. Too far to go."

Malika took another sip of chai. She stared out the window. Her reflection stared back at her. Brown eyes. A pert nose. Long black hair in a neat braid. Not too bad even if she thought so herself. Veer certainly thought so!

Bhangarh Fort would be popular with their fans. If they earned money, she could help at home. Papa had recently been laid off. Ma was working two jobs to pay the bills. And put food on the table. She *had* to do better than them. University abroad. That was her dream!

"What if I pay for fuel and food?" Malika said. She had money from her summer tutoring job. "Can you borrow your dad's car?"

"Why do you want to go so badly?" Veer asked. He frowned. "This is the *third* time you've brought it up."

"Let me show you something," said Malika. She'd known he would need convincing. So she'd done her homework. She wrote a number on a napkin. "Once we get 50,000 fans, VidVibe will put ads on our channel. And this is what we'll make, *every month*!"

Veer's eyes widened. "Is that in rupees or American dollars?"

"Rupees!" Malika said. She rolled her eyes. "We're in India, in case you'd forgotten."

She looked at the number again. American dollars would be sixty times more. A *huge* sum. All her dreams would come true.

"I wouldn't say no to some decent cash for a change," Veer said. "But Bhangarh Fort was in the news just last week. A tourist ran out screaming at midday. She said it was a dangerous place. That it should be shut down. You saw that article, right?"

Malika shrugged. Veer was right. The local newspaper had interviewed the tourist, who was from the UK. The woman said she'd heard sobbing from the palace building. She'd even felt an evil presence there. That story had been picked up by the *Bharat Times* blog. It had over a million views already.

"*Everyone* loves a good ghost story," Malika said. "People grow up with spooky stories. No matter what age, they still love reading them. *We* hunt ghosts. Match made in heaven! Please say yes!"

Veer said nothing. He swirled chai in his clay cup.

"It's the long weekend coming up," Malika said. "Borrow your dad's car. We head out on Saturday. Record all evening and night at Bhangarh Fort. We'll explore the local sights on Sunday. And we're back home on Monday. This is our chance to go big, Veer!"

Veer looked troubled. "They say it's a love story gone badly wrong—"

"Wait!" Malika said. She grabbed her phone. "Say it on camera. Our fans will get a taste of what's to come. Make it exciting. Go!"

Veer looked unsure. But he forced an upbeat tone. "During the seventeenth century there lived a beautiful princess called Rani Ratnavati. And an evil tantrik—"

"Friends, in Hindi *rani* means 'princess' or 'queen.' *Tantrik* means 'magician,'" Malika said, switching the camera view to herself. She turned the camera back to Veer.

Veer continued. "The magician, Singhya, tried to cast a spell on her using a vial of her favorite perfume. The plan backfired somehow. She spurned his love. She threw the vial on a boulder. It rolled over him. Killed him. Before he died, he put a curse on her, on the fort and on the village. The city fell into ruin. She was trapped there forever."

Malika slid in beside Veer. They were both on camera. "Stay tuned, Ghosties! We're going to Bhangarh this weekend!"

Malika switched off her phone. She turned to Veer. "This story has love, hate, anger, revenge and ghosts! If *we* don't do it, someone else will. And we'll have lost out on ad revenue and fans. We could both do with some cash, Veer!"

"Enough already!" Veer said. He shook his head. "I can never say no to you."

Malika snuggled up to him. "Thanks, Veer. You won't regret this! Rani Rat, see you soon."

Veer kissed her. Malika kissed him back tenderly. She'd won, as she'd known she would. When she wanted something, *no one* could stop her.

No one.

Chapter Two

The windshield wipers swished back and forth. Heavy rain had started about an hour earlier. It showed no signs of stopping. Black clouds hung low in a gray sky.

"Man, I *hate* driving in this muck," Veer said. "But Dad would kill me if I let you drive his car."

Malika shrugged. "He doesn't have to know."

"Thanks, but no," Veer said, glancing at her. "Why so quiet?"

"Thinking of the script," she replied. She was scribbling in a notepad. "It'll be closing time when we reach the fort. We'll have to go in quick. Then hide if we plan to spend the night."

"No one is allowed to stay the night," Veer said. "You know that, right?"

"All the more reason to stick around," Malika said. "Bhangarh Fort is one of the *best* tourist attractions. Not just in Rajasthan but in all of India. I think it's a hoax. They might have fog machines. Or recorded sounds to scare tourists. We'll find the truth. And report it to our fans."

"And what if Rani Ratnavati and the tantrik are real?" Veer said. "We'll be trapped with them in the fort all night. Creepy!"

Malika put a hand on his arm. "Relax, Veer.

We'll be in and out before you know it. Also, I need the money. The situation at home isn't too good."

Veer nodded. She'd already told him about her papa losing his job.

They were silent as they drove the last few miles. Malika stared out the window. She watched villages go by. Huts with damp brick walls were plastered with black dung cakes. Pathways had turned to rivers of mud in the rain. A few people, covered in black tarps, still worked in the fields. Oxen plodded along in the pouring rain. The gloomy day was perfect for ghost hunting.

"Made it!" Veer said. He pointed to the fort in the distance. "There's still a couple of hours to closing time."

Malika's heartbeat quickened. Bhangarh Fort had once been a sprawling city. Within the city walls were ruined houses, marketplaces and temples. The main attraction now was the royal palace.

Rani Ratnavati had lived there. The reddish brick walls had crumbled in many places. A row of inverted U-shaped windows lined the tops of the walls. They looked like sightless eyes, watching the road.

The place looked so much spookier than in the pictures. Were they making a mistake by staying the night?

Malika was tempted to turn around. Go back home. She pushed away the thought. They *would* spend one night at the fort.

Content creators took great risks for great rewards. They jumped off cliffs. Some walked on ropes between two skyscrapers, without a safety net. Others ate hot peppers by the hundreds. Their posts went viral, making them rich and famous.

With that kind of money, Malika could secure her future. She could help out at home. And start saving to study abroad. She hated seeing her parents so stressed.

Tonight everything would change. For her and Veer. She was sure of it. She just had to be brave.

Veer parked the car. They gathered their equipment. Malika hurried to buy tickets so they could get out of the rain. Occasional flashes of lightning zigzagged through the sky. The smell of wet earth and rotting leaves hung in the air.

A bored-looking man in a white kurta and jeans perked up when he saw them. "Gates close in two hours. Come back tomorrow. Better value for money."

"That's okay," Malika said. She pulled out her wallet. "We'd like to go in now."

The man shrugged and gave them their tickets. "There's a bad storm tonight. Come back to this gate before 5 p.m. I have to lock up and go home."

"Sure," Malika said. She glanced at Veer. He gave her a warm smile even though he looked worried.

She squeezed his arm. "By tomorrow we'll

have the best footage ever. It will go viral. Mark my words," she whispered. "We're going to be rich!"

They passed through the main gates. As they climbed the stone-paved ramp, Malika felt a deep chill around her. It was as if they'd walked into a meat freezer. Or a cemetery on a winter day. Her heart raced. She took a deep, calming breath. *You can do this. You have to do this.*

"Let's get some footage before we go in," she said. She handed her phone to Veer. "I'll upload it as a teaser. Along with your intro about Rani Rat and Singhya."

"Stop calling her that, M.," Veer said. "It's rude."

Malika rolled her eyes. "Okaaaay!"

She felt an icy draft at the base of her neck. The sky seemed to get darker. She took a deep breath, ignoring her racing heart.

Veer nodded as soon as he was ready.

"Hey, Ghosties, this is the Ghost Queen, Malika, with her trusty knight, Veer," Malika said. "We're recording live from Bhangarh Fort in Rajasthan. We'll bring you the *actual* story of Rani Ratnavati and the evil magician, Singhya, who didn't understand that no means *no*."

She turned to look at the fort. Then back toward the camera, looking serious. "Would *you* spend the night here? Drop us a line in the comments section. We'd love to hear from you. Don't forget to click the *like* and *subscribe* buttons. Wish us luck!"

Veer gave the phone back to Malika. She uploaded the teaser to VidVibe. The Wi-Fi was spotty. It took a couple of minutes. Her hands trembled. Despite a long-sleeved T-shirt and a rain jacket, she was freezing.

What if this was real? She shook her head. Nope. This was all her imagination. And the spooky vibes this place was giving off? Their fans would love it!

Malika consulted the map. She led the way toward the royal palace. That was the best place to start. It was the most popular with the tourists.

It started pouring again. They both raced toward the palace entrance. Inside, it was dark and gloomy. Gray, water-stained walls surrounded them. Leaves tumbled across the damp floor. The dank smell of rotting wood filled Malika's nose. She reached out to steady herself. Quickly she drew back her hand. Even the walls felt slimy.

Facing them was a corridor with high arched doorways. They stretched away into darkness. At regular intervals the corridor opened onto the courtyard.

Even as she watched, a shadow moved in the blackness. It was coming closer. The thump of footsteps echoed around them.

Malika clapped a hand to her mouth to stifle a scream.

Chapter Three

The figure came closer. As soon as Malika saw the uniform, she relaxed.

"You're a police officer," she said. She was annoyed at herself for being so jumpy.

"And *you're* up to no good," the police officer said. Sweat stains spread from his armpits in large damp patches. He looked tired and grubby.

"We're just looking around and taking pictures," Malika said. "What's wrong with that?"

"It's almost closing time," he said. "Come back tomorrow."

"We've paid for the tickets. We're not leaving till we see this place," Veer said. "Please, sir," he added, "we've driven all the way from Delhi."

The police officer seemed to thaw a little. "Tonight's storm will be severe. I will not be on duty. Nor will the ticket seller. If you get into trouble, there'll be no one to help you. Come back to the gate within the hour. Okay?"

"Yes," they said in unison.

The police officer hurried away, looking nervously around him.

"Is he acting? Or is he really scared?" Veer asked. "I hate this already."

"Acting," Malika said. "How else can they convince tourists this place is haunted?"

She saw the police officer hurry across the courtyard. Almost as if someone was chasing him.

Veer was peering into the dark, endless corridor behind her. "Something's moving back there." His voice was a whisper. "Not kidding."

Malika turned around. At first she saw just the corridor. Openings on either side led to the courtyard. Faint light filtered in. But the far end of the corridor was black.

Then she saw it. A shadow moved. Red eyes peered at them. Instinct screamed at her to run. But Malika stood her ground.

The shadow came closer. As soon as it passed an opening, Malika saw it clearly. A mangy, flea-bitten dog. It prowled up to them and stood still, watching them silently.

"Are you getting this on camera?" Malika whispered.

"Yes," Veer replied. "Looks spooky in this light."

"What's it looking at?" Malika asked. "Why isn't it barking?"

The dog suddenly whimpered. It backed away. The hairs on the back of Malika's neck rose. Her skin prickled. She heard a faint sound from the courtyard.

Suddenly there was a huge rumble. The ground shook. Malika and Veer both dashed out of the nearest opening. A brick wall in front of them crumbled inward. No one was around. No one came running. They were all alone.

“How did that happen?” Veer asked. “And what if the fort starts crumbling while we’re *inside*? We should leave, M. Now.”

Malika went back inside. The dog had seen something before it whimpered. Following it might lead them to the ghosts. Or help them expose the hoax.

The animal was gone.

“Did you see where it went?” Malika asked, looking around.

“We didn’t see it come out, so down there is the only option,” Veer said. He jerked his head toward the end of the corridor.

“Let’s go straight to the rani’s chamber,” Malika said. “If there’s going to be any action, this is where it’ll be. In Rani Rat’s chamber.”

"Please *stop* calling her Rani Rat," Veer said. He looked annoyed. "What if sh—someone hears us..." His voice trailed away.

Malika burst into laughter. "Veer, you're killing me. There's no one here. Just hype and stories. Probably special effects to scare the tourists. To make them come back. I'll call her Rani. Okay?"

"Let's just get this over with," Veer said. His eyes darted around. "I hate this place already."

They started down the long corridor. Someone called out to them.

"Hey, Mister, Miss, where are you?" The voice came from the entrance.

"Quick, hide!" Malika said. "It's that police officer. He'll drag us out if he sees us."

They both ducked into a crumbling alcove. Cobwebs brushed Malika's skin. The smell of dead animal was strong. Malika shuddered. She took shallow breaths.

"Friends, come back. It is not safe to spend the night." It was the ticket collector. "Please believe me. You will not live to see tomorrow. Leave now while you can."

Malika squeezed Veer's hand. She rolled her eyes. "Will they stop with the acting already!"

"People have died here! Come back now." It was the police officer again.

"Maybe—" Veer began, but Malika planted a kiss on his lips.

"We have to stay. We can't disappoint our fans now. Not after we put the teaser out there already. I bet there are a ton of likes. Let me check." She tapped her phone. "I've lost cell signal. Not a single bar. You?"

Veer whipped out his phone.

"Same," he said.

An extra-loud of clap of thunder shook the air. The alcove lit up with a burst of lightning. When the sound died away, there was silence. The police officer and ticket guy had left. They were on their own now.

"Headlamps on," Malika said. "Let's go find the rani."

Rubbing the goose bumps on her arms, she led the way.

Chapter Four

They moved deeper into the corridor as night fell. Light filtering in from the openings faded into black.

"This place is a maze," Malika said. She studied the map. "Here's the path to go up to the rani's chambers. It's steep. Watch your step."

Veer adjusted his headlamp to make it brighter. He hoisted the tripod strap on his shoulder and followed Malika. His handheld camera continued to record their progress.

They crossed a courtyard. Banyan-tree roots spilled over low crumbling walls. Leaves rustled in a stiff, cold breeze. Something black zipped by them. Malika almost screamed.

"Ugh!" she said, pressing a hand to her heart. "I hate bats!"

"And dogs!" Veer said. "So many of them."

"We only saw one–" Malika stopped when he gripped her arm.

Malika's headlamp picked up red pinpricks around them.

Dogs, all around.

They stood in the shadows of the walls. They hid behind trees. Watching them. As if waiting for something to happen.

"They're harmless, I'm sure," Malika said. She desperately wanted to be convinced of it.

But these mutts gave her the creeps. "Keep the camera rolling. It will add to the spookiness. I'll amp it up when I do the edits."

They climbed a narrow staircase to the upper level of the royal palace. More crumbling brick walls and then a wide-open sky. It was completely dark now. The only light was from their headlamps.

A faint smell of jasmine perfumed the air. Malika sniffed. *She* wasn't wearing any perfume. Could there be jasmine plants nearby? The smell was heavenly.

A light drizzle had started up again. Drops of icy rain beaded Malika's face. The raindrops looked like silver shards in the light of the headlamps.

"This way," Malika said. "Follow me."

A piercing shriek shattered the silence. Malika jumped. She reached for Veer. She looked up in time to see a magnificent peacock sail by. Its blue-green feathers seemed to glow.

Malika took a deep breath. She faced Veer, who was holding the camera. If she focused on the fans, maybe she would forget to be scared.

"Are you seeing this, Ghosties?" Malika said. "We're steps away from the rani's chambers. So far we've only seen dogs, bats and a peacock. Now to see if there are any ghosts. Where is Rani Rat? And Singhya?"

"Malika," Veer said in a low voice. "You promised not to call her that."

Malika ignored him. "Here's some cool info, Ghosties. Bhangarh Fort is so cursed that if someone even tries to build a home here, it collapses. Many have died here. No one dares attempt it now. This place will remain abandoned forever. And now…to the rani's chamber. It's not far from here."

They hurried along the pathway.

Suddenly Veer tripped and fell. The camera flew from his hands. Malika raced to help him. She cursed under her breath. She breathed a sigh when she saw the camera snagged on a bush. It was still intact!

"That was lucky," she said. She helped Veer to his feet. "Told you to be careful."

"I fell over something soft," Veer whispered. "I bet it was them." He pointed behind Malika.

Out of the darkness they approached. Dogs again. Dozens of them. Red eyes watching their every move. Mouths drooling saliva. Open sores covered their thin bodies.

"What do we do?" Malika asked. She felt sick. "Make a run for it?"

"NO!" Veer said. He grabbed her hand. "Rabies. Can't risk being bitten. Back away slowly. No sudden moves."

"It's almost as if they don't want us to go into the rani's chamber," Malika whispered.

"We should take the hint and *leave*," Veer said. He slung the camera around his neck.

"No!" Malika said. "We've come too far to stop now." If they did, goodbye, cool footage. Goodbye, new fans. Goodbye, money.

Ma's tired face flashed into her head. Malika's dream to go abroad would be down the toilet. She *had* to go on.

Three dogs came closer. Malika and Veer took a step back.

The air turned frigid. Malika's breath fogged in front of her face. Suddenly a foul stink overpowered the smell of jasmine flowers. The stink of something long dead.

"Ugh!" Malika covered her nose with her sleeve.

"Why are the dogs so quiet?" Veer said. "Something's spooked them."

As if on cue, the dogs whined. They backed away. One by one, they melted into the shadows. Malika froze.

The dogs had been terrified. Something was there. Something Malika and Veer couldn't see yet. Special effects couldn't fool animals. For the first time, Malika felt her stomach churn. Her hands were cold and clammy. Were they finally going to see the ghosts?

"You should not be here," someone whispered behind them. It was a man's deep voice. He sounded cold and cruel.

Malika flung herself at Veer as creepy laughter echoed around them.

Chapter Five

As abruptly as it had started, the laughter stopped. Nothing moved. Cold rain pattered down on the stones. It slid down their necks. They shivered. No other sound disturbed the eerie silence. Even the stink was gone.

"Show yourself, coward!" Malika yelled. "We're not scared." Her voice trembled. Veer hugged her closer. His hand and the camera trembled.

They seemed to be alone. Yet Malika felt something evil was around. *Watching* them. Just like that tourist had described it.

"This was a bad idea!" Veer said. "I can feel it. Something foul. Let's go. *Now*!"

Malika wanted to leave too, but she knew she had to go on. For Ma and Papa. And for herself. There was a story here. And she was *this* close. To give up now would be foolish. She knew she wouldn't have the courage to come back here again.

Malika took a deep breath. "I'm staying. The rani's chamber is right there. At the end of this path."

"Come on, M.," Veer said. "This is dangerous. We've already got enough footage. We can always say we stayed the night. Say we didn't see anything."

"I won't lie to my fans," Malika said. She desperately wanted to run. But the need to make money was stronger. Veer didn't know the full story. She was afraid he'd break up with her if he found out her family was flat broke.

"*Our* fans," Veer said. "So you'd rather ignore the danger? I hate this place. I want out."

"We're steps from the rani's chamber," Malika said. "I need footage of the inside. Then we'll leave, I promise. Please. Just one minute."

Veer was silent. Malika sent up a silent prayer. She hoped he would stick with her.

This place scared the hell out of her. She didn't know if she could do it if Veer left.

"All right," Veer said finally. "One minute. You heard that voice. It was real, no matter what you say."

They hurried along the narrow path. A fierce wind whipped by. Rain poured down. Within seconds they reached the rani's chamber. It was small, with three open doorways. Malika stepped inside.

The wall facing the entrance was covered with graffiti. A high ceiling was set with stone carvings of birds and animals. It was chipped and cracked but there were no holes. It gave some shelter from the heavy rain.

Veer looked around. "Sad place for a princess," he said.

"Do you smell jasmine?" Malika asked. "The story says Singhya put a spell on a vial of perfume. The rani's favorite. It was jasmine."

"How can the smell be lingering after 400 years?" Veer asked. "Odd!"

"Listen!" Malika said. "Hear that?"

Veer fell silent. It was so soft, Malika thought she was mistaken. Soon, it grew louder. Malika looked around her.

At first she saw nothing. Then suddenly the outline of a ghost appeared in the corner. It was a woman in a white outfit. She sat on the floor. Her head was tucked into her knees.

Malika slid her hand into Veer's. Like hers, it was clammy. Her heart slammed against her rib cage.

The rani was here! Malika nudged Veer. He raised the camera. As soon as he pressed the *record* button, a red light came on. Rani Ratnavati looked up. Her face was bony. Rotting. The chamber echoed with her shriek.

"GET OUT!"

It was a cry filled with pain and anger. "I'm sick of you peasants coming to stare at my chamber. To enjoy my pain! Singhya, let me go! I beg of you. Let me go!"

It was so loud and piercing that Malika clapped her hands to her ears. Veer froze, his face bloodless as he flattened himself against the far wall.

Wind howled through the chamber. It churned up dust and dead leaves. It grew so cold, their teeth chattered.

"Never, my love!" a deep and cruel voice boomed from outside. "We'll be together for eternity!"

It was the same voice that had whispered behind them earlier.

Malika and Veer backed out of the chamber. They raced out the way they'd come. Malika couldn't help but look back. The ghost of the rani beat her hands against the wall. She was still sobbing.

A gigantic man stood beside the chamber. A flash of lightning illuminated him. He was bald, with a twisted, angry face. A straggly black beard hung over his chest. Necklaces of skulls, big and small, were draped over him. Three white stripes were painted across his forehead.

It could be none other than Singhya. Black eyes without pupils bored into Malika. For a moment she was frozen in place. Veer stood frozen beside her.

The rani sobbed.

"Silence!" Singhya snapped.

Rani Ratnavati fell silent.

Singhya glared at Malika and Veer. "You should not be here. You have made a grave mistake."

His shadow flew toward them, a foul-smelling black cloud.

"RUN!" Malika screamed.

Chapter Six

They ran down the stairs. Somehow they made it back to the ground floor. The corridor leading to the main gate stretched out before them. It was a black void. They hurried toward it. They dodged holes, roots and stones. Rain had puddled on the floor. It was slippery.

"Leaving so soon?" boomed a terrifying yet familiar voice. It was close. Too close. "Stay forever. Keep my Ratnavati company."

Malika screamed as Singhya materialized in front of her. Her headlamp lit up his eyes. They looked like twin black holes. The skulls on his necklace clicked and clattered.

Veer grabbed Malika's hand. He pulled her toward one of the openings in the corridor. Just as they reached it, a mangy dog appeared. It bared its teeth, red eyes boring into them.

They backed away. Malika's heart thundered in her chest. It drowned out the snarls of the dog. She was in danger of passing out. She dug her fingernails into her palms. The pain helped. A little.

"This way," Veer whispered. He tugged Malika along.

Thank God he still has his wits about him, Malika thought.

They hurried to another opening in the corridor. Another dog barred the way.

Behind them Singhya roared with laughter. "There is no escape. Stay, Malika. My Ratnavati could use a friend. The other one is not needed."

Suddenly he was in their faces. He leered at them. Chapped black lips parted to show a hedge of yellow, broken teeth. Singhya's breath was foul, as though something dead was in his mouth. His eyes like oily pools were fixed on them. Malika felt like she was drowning.

There was a cry from somewhere in the distance. "Singhya!"

"Ratnavati needs me," Singhya said. He whirled and disappeared up the stairs.

"Bless the rani," Veer said. "Let's get out before he comes back."

"How?" Malika asked. "Those dogs won't let us."

Veer grabbed a rock. He hurled it at the nearest dog. The mutt growled and sidestepped it. The others closed in. No matter where they went, the dogs followed. More appeared from the shadows. Like the hounds of hell. There seemed to be no escape.

The storm was worse than ever. Rain gusted in. They were getting soaked to the skin. Lightning tore through the sky. The wind howled like an animal in pain.

"What if we go farther into the palace? Find a different exit?" Malika said.

"Anything is worth a try," Veer said grimly. "Go!" He turned his headlamp to the highest setting. They clambered over piles of rubble, heading in the opposite direction. Suddenly the ground shook again. A massive boulder landed in front of them. It blocked their way.

Malika screamed. Veer pulled her back just in time. Ashen-faced, they stared at each other. Malika knew this was no accident. No matter where they went, a rabid dog or falling stone barred their way.

Exhausted, Malika sat on the stone steps. Her breath came in painful gasps. She was close to bawling. "I'm so sorry I suggested this, Veer!"

"No time for that now," said Veer. "Let's head back up. We might find another way out. Do you still have the map?"

Malika shook her head mournfully. "I must have dropped it."

"Never mind," Veer said. "Let's just go." He took the memory card out of the camera and slipped it into Malika's hand. Then he dropped the tripod and camera. "Don't want anything slowing us down."

Malika raced up the steps. Veer was right behind her.

There was an ominous rumble. Malika looked up. A crack lashed across the ceiling above them. They dove apart just as the stone ceiling caved in.

When the dust cleared, Malika got to her feet. She coughed. "Veer, I'm okay. You?"

Silence.

"VEER!" He couldn't be dead. She'd never forgive herself.

Malika heard a soft moan. Relief flooded her. She scrambled over the debris. Veer lay at the bottom of the stairs. His left leg was pinned under a large slab of stone. But he was alive! Blood oozed from a gash on his head. His face was covered with dust.

"Get help," he whispered. His eyes rolled back.

Malika tried to move the stone, but it was too heavy for her. After a few tries, she stopped.

There was only one thing to do. Confront Rani Ratnavati and Singhya. And plead that they let her and Veer go. She'd promise not to use the footage she'd taken. Anything to get out of here.

Chapter Seven

Malika climbed the steps. Her heartbeat thundered in her ears. Rain pounded the exposed upper level. The smell of wet earth mingled with the sweet smell of jasmine. The first time she'd smelled it, she'd loved it. Now it made her want to vomit.

Within seconds she was drenched despite the rain jacket. Slipping and sliding along the muddy path, she made her way toward the rani's chamber.

Her headlamp was waterproof. It lit up Rani Ratnavati, a transparent figure in a long-sleeved tunic and a white brocade skirt that fell to her feet. Her hair looked like a black waterfall down her back. The ghost seemed to be waiting for her in a corner of the chamber.

Malika whimpered as the rani suddenly stood in front of her. Her decayed flesh quivered as she asked, "Who are you?"

"M-M-Malika. My name is Malika."

"You call me Rani Rat," the ghost said. "Not very respectful, is it?"

Malika swallowed. Her mouth was so dry, she almost choked. Up close the smell of jasmine was overpowering. "I'm sorry," she said. "I was shortening your very long name, but I meant no disrespect. Please forgive me, Rani Ratnavati. Please let me—let us go."

The rani drew herself up. "What brings you to my cursed palace? My tomb? Fame? Wealth? Curiosity? Speak up. Do not lie to me. I will know if you do."

Malika shuddered at the anger in the rani's voice. "It's not like that at all," she said. "Veer and I have a content channel—a kind of show—called *Ghost Queen*. We thought the haunting of Bhangarh Fort was just a ploy to get tourists. We—*I* was wrong. I didn't mean to disturb you. I'm sorry!"

Rani Ratnavati seemed to ponder this.

"This ghost queen. It is you?" she asked.

"Yes," Malika said. "Sort of."

“And Veer,” Rani said thoughtfully. “He is the handsome boy with you?”

“Yes. My...friend. My boyfriend.”

Rani moved away. She stood at the entrance, gazing out over her city. “I can see this is the truth. I might even forgive you. But Singhya is a brute. He’ll never let you go.”

Malika went numb with terror. Somehow she had to convince the rani to help her and Veer escape.

“Is there anything I can do to help you?” Malika asked. “That is, if you help us get out of here.” Staring into that decayed face made her want to vomit. But she didn’t dare offend the rani anymore. Not if she wanted to get out. Alive.

"Malika and Rani Ratnavati," said the rani. She still stared into the distance. "Both ghost queens. Almost sisters."

Malika saw zero resemblance between them. One of them had been dead for 400 years. But she wasn't going to say that.

"In that case, won't you please forgive your sister? Won't you let us go?" Malika said. "Singhya has us trapped. With his dogs." Malika's voice broke at the thought of that rabid pack still down there, waiting for them.

The rani sighed. "I understand being trapped. Do you know how terrible it is to be locked in here for eternity? With a monster who still lusts after me?" She seemed not to have heard Malika's plea.

Malika could almost imagine Ratnavati as a beautiful young woman with a bright future. With hopes and dreams. Malika understood that.

"I'm sorry. I wish I could help, but I can't," Malika said. "But at least *you* can help us. Maybe you can distract Singhya while we make a run for it? We all heard you call out to him earlier. Where is he now?"

Rani Ratnavati smiled. It made Malika shudder. "I drew him away to another part of the palace so we could speak."

"We need to go before he gets back," Malika said. "Help us, and I'll help you. Maybe I can find a way to break the curse. To set you free."

The rani sighed. "Singhya is the most powerful tantrik of all time. But"—she smiled slyly—"I have learned a few things in my 400 years as a doomed spirit. And one secret I recently learned gives me hope."

Malika had zero desire to know what the rani had learned. "I have to go, Rani Ratnavati. Is Singhya close?"

"Not yet, but he's coming," the rani said. "With gifts and sweet words to wear me down. He cannot touch me without my permission. But to be wooed by the *wrong* man, for *eternity*, is a fate for the truly wicked."

Malika's heart ached for this woman. But *was* she wicked? Or had she been in the wrong place at the wrong time?

Rani Ratnavati drifted toward one of the open doorways. "This chamber was my sanctuary. Now it is my prison. How I ache to be free." She suddenly whirled around. Her hand shot out and grasped Malika's wrist. Malika's skin burned, but her insides felt icy. She snatched her hand away.

Rani Ratnavati smiled coldly. "We are sisters, you and I. By name and by deeds. You're brave and strong. I felt it when I touched you. No woman has dared spend the night in the palace. You are the first in 400 years. Stay. Keep me company. There is much I can tell you."

"Thanks, but no thanks," Malika said. Sweat pooled in her armpits.

They both heard the voice at the same time. "My love, I have returned. Did you miss me?"

Malika's heart stuttered in her chest. Rani Ratnavati was scary. But Singhya was pure evil. She peeked over the parapet wall. The voice came from the courtyard below. The gauzy outline of Singhya's ghost moved through the fort. He was taking his time, making them sweat.

A sob escaped the rani's lips. She turned her decayed face to Malika. "No reason why we should both suffer. I shall be merciful. RUN!"

Malika jumped through the doorway and onto the path. Singhya's footsteps echoed on the bare floor below, growing louder. She hurried along the muddy path to the stairway. Veer was somewhere at the bottom, still pinned under the stone. They had to get away.

Suddenly something slammed into her.

Malika felt as if she'd fallen into an icy lake. She couldn't breathe. She clawed at her throat. She gasped for air. There seemed to be none.

Images, sounds and smells surrounded her. Singhya leering. Rani Ratnavati cowering. The smell of jasmine. The stink of a carcass. Sobs, harsh words and pleas.

She was falling. Falling. Falling.

Into darkness and utter silence.

Chapter Eight

"Malika! Talk to me! Are you okay?"

Veer kept calling her name. Finally she woke up. She looked dazed.

"What happened?" she asked. Her voice sounded hoarse, strange.

"You fell down the stairs. You okay? Anything broken?"

His leg was killing him. And he was trapped. Until someone moved the stone slab, there was no leaving this cursed place.

At least it was getting lighter. Maybe the police officer and the ticket collector would be back soon. They would help. Malika looked to be in no condition to even stand up.

"I'm...okay," she mumbled. Suddenly she leaned over and retched. Black vomit gushed out. She shuddered and wiped her mouth with the back of her hand.

Veer tried not to show his disgust. The vomit smelled of rotten meat. What had Malika eaten that smelled so gross?

"See if the ticket guy or the police officer have arrived," Veer said. "Get them to help move this stone."

Malika got to her feet. She swayed on the

spot for a second or two. Then she seemed to recover. She stumbled and slipped. But she made her way over to him.

"I'm going to free you, my handsome Veer. I'm not leaving you here alone. Not with that brute Singhya."

Malika was talking weird, Veer thought. It could just be the aftereffects of meeting the ghosts.

"I don't think you can move a rock almost as heavy as you—" He stopped.

Malika was moving the massive rock as if it were a football.

Veer watched her, aghast. His leg was badly bruised and bleeding. But he could still move it. It was a miracle that no bones were broken.

"You did it, M.!" Veer sat up. "Do you know how much I love you?"

Malika smiled. She helped him stand. Weak morning light filtered into the corridor. In the gloom, her brown eyes looked almost black. He shook his head. The light was playing tricks on him.

"Let's go!" he said. "I've had enough of this place."

"That makes two of us," Malika said.

They hurried down the gloomy corridor. Mangy dogs milled at the entrance. They growled.

"They won't let us go! We're trapped!" Veer said. He almost wanted to break down and sob.

Malika stooped and picked up a rock. She

flung it at the nearest dog. The rock landed on its snout. The dog yelped. It backed away.

"SHOO!" Malika said.

The rest of them fled.

"Why didn't they do that last night?" Veer asked.

"Who cares?" Malika said. "Let's just go. I never want to see this place again. Not as long as I live."

"Same here," Veer said. He leaned on her shoulder. They hobbled to the parking lot in silence.

When they reached the car, Malika stared at it like she was seeing it for the first time. Veer limped to the passenger side. He opened the door. "Get in."

Malika slid into the seat. She looked bewildered. He had to remind her to put on her seat belt. He even helped her with it.

Shock. That was all it was, thought Veer as he limped to the driver's side. "I can still drive. Dad will be mad at me if I let you drive."

Malika looked straight ahead as he drove away. He thought he could hear her humming softly under her breath. He wasn't sure.

Veer gripped the gearshift. Malika slid her hand over his. Her fingers were ice-cold. But who cared? They had survived Bhangarh Fort. A place he'd dreaded. It felt good to have faced his fear. And Malika had been amazing.

"You were so brave," Veer said.

"Keep talking," Malika said, giving him a

sly look. "I love compliments from beautiful boys."

Veer frowned at the road. That was an odd thing for Malika to say. He didn't know how to respond.

"You still have that memory card I gave you, right?" Veer asked after a moment.

Malika looked confused. Like she'd forgotten where she'd put it.

"In your pocket," he said.

She dug it out with her free hand. "This?"

"Keep it safe," Veer said. "It'll be a hit with our fans. Your money problems are over. I guarantee it."

Malika smiled. She tucked the card back into her pocket.

When the fort was no longer visible in the rearview mirror, Veer relaxed a bit. Malika seemed to relax too. She let go of Veer's hand.

With slow movements, she undid her long braid. She shook out the wavy strands. Veer glanced over, admiring her. Malika never wore her hair loose. It was lovely, falling like a black waterfall down her back and shoulders.

A faint scent of jasmine suddenly filled the car. Malika turned. She gave Veer a warm, inviting smile.

Veer sighed. He was more in love with her than ever before.

Chapter Nine

Malika opened her eyes. She was lying at the foot of the stairs. The sky outside was lighter. Dawn was approaching. Every bone in Malika's body ached.

What had happened? She remembered running away. Something had slammed into her. She'd heard yells, pleas. Then nothing.

She must have fallen down the stairs. Been knocked out.

She was more angry than scared. When she got out of here, she would go straight to the police station. She'd recommend that Bhangarh Fort be torn down.

If they didn't listen, she'd come back with friends and do it herself. Or start an online petition. No one else would go through what she and Veer had. This place really was dangerous.

"Veer?" she called out.

No response.

Malika got to her feet. Her head pounded. Her vision was blurry. No one was around. Had Veer left? But he'd been pinned under a rock, so how could he have left?

The rain had stopped. Puddles in the corridor reflected a pale pink sky. Malika hobbled toward the nearest opening leading to the courtyard. Once she was outside, she'd circle back to the ticket counter and call for help.

"Veer!" she called out again.

No answer except her own voice echoing through the ruins.

Fear gave her the strength to move faster. As she tried to slip through the opening, she felt a sharp tug at her navel. It seemed as if a thin invisible line was holding her back. She tried again. The pain was too intense. She had to stop.

She looked down, suddenly realizing two things. She was wearing the outfit that Rani Ratnavati had been wearing. And someone was behind her.

Malika turned. For the first time, she saw the tantrik clearly. Inhumanly tall, with a bald, bony head, black, pupil-less eyes and a thick black beard. He leered at her. He licked his lips. It sent chills up her spine.

"My love, will you never stop trying to escape?" Singhya said. "I've told you again and again. The curse I put on this fort, and on you, means that you can *never* leave. Not unless *I* set you free. And that will never happen. We're in this together. Forever."

Malika's blood froze. What was he talking about? Could he not see she wasn't his dead love but a living human? The rani must have played a trick on her. She'd dressed Malika in her own clothes.

Singhya came closer. His lewd gaze undressed her. A horrible thought struck her. She looked down at the puddle below her feet. At her reflection in the water.

The decayed face of Rani Ratnavati stared up at her. A sob burst out of her mouth. *Now* she understood what had happened.

Rani Ratnavati had stolen her body! Her life.

The future she'd dreamed of.

And Veer.

Singhya reached out for her with scarred hands. His overgrown yellow nails looked like talons. Malika turned and ran. She screamed and sobbed. She knew it was futile. But she ran anyway.

No one had been able to stop her when she wanted something.

Until now.

Acknowledgments

I'm deeply grateful to my editor, Gabrielle Prendergast, for her invaluable insights to make this story shine. Thanks to my agent, Naomi Davis, who has been supportive and encouraging, and who always gets my work. Lastly, thank you, dear Reader. Because of you, I continue to write.

Mahtab Narsimhan is an award-winning author of over twenty critically acclaimed books in the fantasy, horror, mystery and contemporary genres, and she is also published internationally. Mahtab writes for all age groups, and many of her books have been shortlisted for numerous awards, including the Silver Birch Award, Red Maple Award and the CLA Book of the Year for Children Award. *The Third Eye*, her debut novel, won the Silver Birch Fiction Award in 2009. She is deeply committed to representation and inclusivity in her work. Please visit mahtabnarsimhan.com/ for more information and connect with her on X @MahtabNarsimhan.